BOOK 1

To Alexei

BOOK 1

by
CONNOR HOOVER

Wizards of Tomorrow Book 1

Paperback ISBN: 978-1982089634

For Xena, for unending enthusiasm and energy

CHAPTER 1

Noah's mom didn't even wait until he got in the front door. "Don't forget all your chores," she hollered.

Chores! On the first day of Spring Break. As if that didn't stink enough, outside a giant boom of thunder echoed in the sky. Noah tossed his huge binder on the kitchen table and pretended he didn't hear her. Instead he grabbed a bag of chips from the pantry and ran for his room. If he was quick enough, she wouldn't see him.

But his mom was like a spider. She must've had eight eyes because she saw everything, and she got scary when she was mad. Three steps up and there she was, standing at the top of the stairs, between him and his bedroom door.

"And your room," his mom said. "You were supposed to clean it two weeks ago. The dust is five inches thick."

His phone buzzed with an incoming text. He didn't dare look or she'd go into angry spider mode.

"I'll clean it now," Noah said. "I promise."

"Not yet," she said. "I need you downstairs in ten minutes to help me fold laundry."

Noah would have bet a million dollars that none of his friends had to spend spring break folding laundry. But he did what he always did. He smiled and nodded and said, "Perfect! I'll be down."

That worked. It normally did. His mom stepped to the side, and Noah dashed past her. With luck, she'd forget all about laundry and chores and anything that had to do with dusting. Dusting was the worst.

Noah shut his bedroom door and finally checked his text. It was from his friend Sophia.

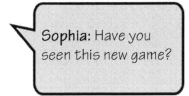

Sophia: Have you seen this new game?

Noah: What game?

Sophia: 'Wizards of Tomorrow.' I'll send you the link.

The name, *Wizards of Tomorrow*, sounded pretty cool, but then she was sending him the link to a new game every other day. Sophia wanted to be a test player for video games when she grew up, so she played as many as she possibly could hoping that would build her job résumé. The last game she'd sent had turned out to be so boring, he fell asleep while playing.

3

Soon enough, the link came through. He clicked on it and installed it. But it took forever, at least two of the ten minutes he had before laundry duty. The second it finished, he clicked *Open*. His phone screen turned bright blue and little gems started bouncing around on the screen. Then they came together and formed the words *Wizards of Tomorrow*. He tapped the screen and he was in.

He was a tiny little figure in the center of the screen, decked out in a cool blue wizard robe with light blue drops on it that almost looked like rain. Except not the dull gray rain like it was doing outside now. Instead, these raindrops were sparkly and glowed, and he used his finger to move his character around.

A text message box popped up on the bottom of the screen.

Sophia: What color is your wizard?

He tapped the message box and the keyboard appeared.

Noah: Blue. What about you?

Sophia: Cool! Mine's red.

He could actually talk to Sophia inside the game. That was pretty awesome.

Noah: What are we supposed to do?

Sophia: There's an empty keyhole at the top of the screen.

Sophia: We have to find a key.

Noah hadn't even noticed the keyhole, but it made complete sense. When it came to video games, Sophia was always right. And if she wasn't right, Noah had learned that arguing with her wasn't always the best idea. So he started moving around the screen and onto the next screens looking for a key. He started on a green background, but as soon as he moved off the top of the screen, the entire thing re-oriented, and he found himself in a castle made of a bunch of tiny little stones. Except the castle was falling apart, like it was old ruins that he was in.

At the top of the new screen was a table, and sitting on the table was the key.

Noah: Found it!

Sophia: Me too!

That was almost too easy. He moved his wizard character to the top of the screen right in front of the table.

He was going to get it first. Noah tapped the screen, right on the key.

The entire screen went blank.

No wait. It wasn't the screen that went blank. It was the entire world around him. Like he was sitting in his bedroom one second and the very next second, everything in his room had turned gray. The world was gone.

CHAPTER 2

Noah tried not to panic as he looked around the gray world. And then he realized that the world wasn't really gray. Instead of the blue walls of his bedroom, wherever he was, the walls were made of gray stones. And the floor was dull wood that was so old it also looked gray. And everything hadn't disappeared. He still held his phone in his hands. Of course, the screen was completely gray.

Noah tapped the screen and the keyboard popped up along with the text box.

Noah: Did something weird happen?

That was simple enough. If this entire thing was a dream, as least he wouldn't look crazy.

Sophia: Weird like the world vanished?

Okay, so something weird was going on. Noah wasn't sure whether her confirming it helped matters or made their situation worse.

Noah: Yeah. Like that.

He stood up because apparently he was sitting on a chair here (wherever here was) just like he had been back in his bedroom. And just like his bedroom, this place had a door.

The more he looked around, the more he was able to figure out what had happened. This must be some kind of virtual reality game. Like he was seeing his room except it looked dingy and run-down. If his mom thought he needed to clean his room for real, she should see this place. His room was immaculate compared to the virtual world.

Noah walked to the giant wooden door and opened it. Outside was a hallway with at least ten other doors that looked exactly like the one he'd come through. And at the end of the hallway was a staircase leading down. Noah started down the stairs, but stopped halfway when he heard noises coming from down below. He crept the rest of the way, finally reaching the bottom and peeking around the corner.

"Sophia!" he said.

"Noah, have you checked this place out?" Sophia said. If she was surprised to see him here at all, she didn't show it.

He spun around and looked. They were in some kind of giant room that looked like it was part of a castle, really similar to the castle in the video game he'd been playing only minutes before. And just like in the video game, the castle was completely falling apart. Like spider webs hung from the ceiling and the stones that made up the walls were chipped and the roof had huge holes in it, letting rain fall through. It was raining here just like it had been back in the real world.

"Is this a virtual reality place?" Noah asked.

Sophia shook her head and walked over to a giant fireplace. "It can't be. No virtual reality is this good. And I've tried all of them."

"Then what happened?" Noah asked, following her over to the fireplace. Like everything else, the mantel above it was caked in at least an inch of dust and grime. His mom would have expected him to stop whatever he was doing and dust it.

"I'll tell you exactly what happened," a voice said from behind them.

Noah and Sophia turned to look.

Two kids they'd never seen before stood there.

The boy took a few steps forward. "I'm Mason. And I know exactly what happened."

The girl stepped up to join him. They looked an awful lot alike, like maybe they were twins.

"You act like you know everything, Mason," the girl said.

"You act like you know everything, Ava," Mason said. "And for your information, I do know what happened here."

Ava, the girl, put her hands on her hips. "What?"

"We got sucked into the video game," Sophia said before Mason could say another word.

"Who are you?" Mason said, eyeing her skeptically.

"Sophia," she said. "And this is Noah. And I think the same thing happened to all of us. Why? What were you going to say?"

Mason shrugged like he didn't care. "Same thing. Sucked into the video game."

Sophia held up her phone. "We all downloaded the app. We all played the game. And we all found the key. Right?"

All four of them nodded.

"So how do we get back?" Noah asked, because all the dust and dirt and spider webs reminded him that if he didn't start folding laundry in the next two minutes, his mom was going to go into full-on rage mode. He looked to Sophia because if anyone was going to have the answer, it would be her.

"I dunno," she said.

"Oh, I bet I do," Ava said.

Mason shook his head. "You don't even play video games. How do you know?"

Ava rolled her eyes. "Because I'm smart. And observant, unlike you."

She walked away from them, back across the room, to where a wooden table sat against a wall.

"Is that a . . . ?" Sophia started saying.

"Yep," Ava said. "It's a key."

She held up a bright gold skeleton key and smiled. "Now we just have to find out what to do with it."

"We open something with it," Mason said, trying to get the key from her.

"What, genius?" Ava said. "Because I don't see a door around here."

But Noah was already moving, back to the other side of the room, near the fireplace. He pulled the tapestry to the side. There behind it was a giant wooden door.

In the center of the door was a keyhole.

CHAPTER 3

va ran over and shoved the golden key into the keyhole. She turned it and the wooden door swung open. The hinges made a huge screeching sound, like the door hadn't been opened in a hundred years. Except that was impossible because in the center of the room behind the door was a round table. And in one of the chair sat a man.

"Oh, I knew you four would find it!" the man said, and he clasped his hands together like he was going to win a prize or something for being right.

Sophia stepped forward and put her hands on her hips. "Find what?"

The man motioned around the place. "This room. The castle. The key."

Noah stepped up beside Sophia to get a better look at the man. He wasn't old, maybe in his twenties, and had dark hair. He wore glasses with dark circular frames that made his eyes look almost like an owl.

"I think he's part of the game," Noah said to Sophia under his breath.

"Part of the game," the man said. "No way. You have it wrong."

"How is that wrong?" Noah said.

"Because I'm not part of the game," the man said. "I am the game."

Mason and Ava stepped forward so all four kids were now in a line, staring the man down. But before anyone could say anything else, the man pointed to the table.

"Sit down. I'll explain everything to you."

Sure enough, there were four more chairs at the round table. And since Noah wanted to know what this guy meant about being the game, he sat.

"Who are you?" Mason said. He said right next to Ava, as if even though they seemed to argue a whole bunch, he wanted to make sure he could protect her in

15

case this guy turned out to be crazy. Noah soon found out that he was crazy.

"My name's Quinn," the guy said. "And I should clarify. When I say that I am the game, what I really mean is that I made the game."

"You designed *Wizards of Tomorrow*?" Sophia said, and for a second her eyes got really big, like she was in complete awe of Quinn.

"Sure did," Quinn said. "Designed the game and enabled it so that you four could come here."

"To this castle?" Ava said.

"To the future," Quinn said.

None of the four kids said a word as Quinn's remark sank in. But finally, after almost a minute of silence, Noah spoke up.

"What exactly do you mean by 'To the future'?" Noah said. "You mean like virtual reality is the future of gaming?" There had been lots of advertising about virtual reality that said just that.

But Quinn shook his head. "This isn't virtual reality. This is the real world. And when I say the future, I mean the future. As in five hundred years in the future."

"So you're saying that we're actually in the future?" Mason said.

"You're lying," Ava said.

"I'm not." Quinn placed both his hands on the table and blew out a deep breath. "Maybe it would be best if I just told you exactly what's going on, from the beginning."

"What a great idea," Ava said. "Maybe if you'd started that way, we'd believe you."

"Oh, you'll believe me," Quinn said. "And then you'll understand why I had no choice."

"No choice in what?" Noah said.

"Shhhh . . . ," Sophia said, placing a finger to her lips. "Just let him talk."

And so Quinn started talking.

"Right, so this all started about five hundred years ago, give or take a decade," Quinn said. "That's when Chaos first appeared."

"Chaos first appeared?" Mason said. "What kind of chaos?"

"Chaos the evil wizard," Quinn said.

Noah couldn't help the smile that crept onto his face. This Quinn guy was taking role playing way seriously. He would have been perfect for a *Dungeons and Dragons* group. But Quinn didn't smile. Neither did Sophia. She was hooked on his every word.

"An evil wizard appeared five hundred years ago?" Ava said. "What? Like he just showed up on the streets and started telling everyone he was a wizard?"

"Stop asking questions," Mason said. "Just let the man talk."

So Quinn went on.

"Right. So five hundred years ago, this evil wizard named Chaos showed up. It was about twenty years after your current time."

"So twenty years in our future," Sophia said.

Quinn nodded. "He showed up. And he started using magic to bring monsters back into the world. One by one, his monsters started to appear. They terrorized the world. The monsters had children, and those monster children also terrorized the world. And before anyone could stop him, nearly all of humanity was gone."

"Like the monster apocalypse?" Noah said. This all still sounded like a big joke, but a creative one.

"Exactly like the monster apocalypse," Quinn said. "Technology was gone. Skyscrapers were gone. Cities were gone. Governments were gone. The world fell apart, and what humans were left went into hiding to stay safe from the monsters that ruled everything. They moved around and tried to survive. Tried to stay hidden, because being seen by the monsters meant death. And death meant complete extinction of humans."

"So what happened?" Mason said. He leaned forward like he didn't want to miss a word.

Noah didn't want to miss a word either. This would be a great idea for his next creative writing paper he had to write for school.

"Well, remember Chaos?" Quinn said.

The kids nodded.

"He used magic to control the monsters. But the problem was that magic didn't exist . . . at least not at first. But maybe it was the monsters or maybe it was Chaos himself, but little by little magic began to appear in the world. Slowly, some of the humans that were left began to develop special powers. Powers over the four elements: fire, water, earth, and air. They could do small things at first, like make the wind blow or start a campfire, but soon, their powers grew. They kept their magic secret, and they planned, and then, from among them, four wizards were chosen, each the best in their special area of magic. And they set out on a secret mission, and they captured and trapped the monsters one by one, until none were left."

"Trapped the monsters how?" Ava said.

Man, she was skeptical. Couldn't she just go along with the story and enjoy it? Noah couldn't wait to see how it ended.

"I'll get to that," Quinn said. "Remind me if I forget. But they trapped the monsters, and they captured Chaos, and only then could humans rebuild their society."

"That's awesome," Mason said. "So they built this place, with castles and cool stuff like that?"

Quinn snapped his fingers. "Exactly! The world got rebuilt. There were castles and governments and trading, and soon the world had another chance. But . . . "

There was always a 'but.' Noah knew it. Every time he asked his mom for something, she came up with some extra clause to tack on to the end of it. 'You can play computer, but . . .' 'You can go to Sophia's house, but . . .' No matter what he asked for, there was always a 'but.'

Noah crossed his arms. "Here it comes," he said.

"Here it comes," Quinn confirmed. "Because in the new world, the rebuilt world, magic was lost."

"You can't just lose magic," Ava said.

"Five hundred years is a long time," Quinn said. "People didn't have a need to use magic and they forget how to do it. And fewer and fewer people were born with the ability to control the four elements. And pretty soon, nobody could do magic at all."

"Except you?" Sophia said, almost hopefully.

Quinn shook his head. "Not even me. As it stands right now, nobody here in the future can use magic."

Mason laughed. "Well it's a good thing those monsters were captured," he said. "Otherwise you guys would be in a whole bunch of trouble."

"About that," Quinn said. "Remember when I said for you to remind me to tell you how the wizards trapped the monsters? How come none of you reminded me?"

"Because you just told us that like two seconds ago," Ava said. "We didn't have a chance."

"I'm reminding you now," Noah said. "How did wizards trap the monsters?"

Quinn blew out a deep breath. "They created something called the Octolith. Beautiful piece of both magic and craftsmanship."

"Octolith," Mason said. "That means eight, right?"

Quinn nodded. "Exactly. The Octolith was a circular stone with eight crystals embedded around the edges. Each crystal was a different color and was used to capture and hold a monster. And in the middle was a pure white crystal. This was the last one created, and the one that required the most magic."

"What monster was in there?" Noah asked. He loved this monster talk. Monsters were the coolest.

"It wasn't a monster," Quinn said. "It was Chaos himself."

"The evil wizard?" Noah said. "They captured the evil wizard in a crystal?"

"Yep," Quinn said. "Chaos was in the center and the eight monsters he revived were in the eight surrounding crystals."

"That's awesome," Mason said. "Do we get to see this Octo-thing?"

"Octolith," Quinn said. "And yes. It's actually right here."

He twisted the giant round table about a foot, and the entire surface of the table shifted. All four kids leaned back, taking their hands off the table. It transformed into a giant carved stone. But instead of eight crystals around the edges, like Quinn had said, there were eight empty sockets, as if the crystals were missing. And instead of a pure white crystal in the middle, there was a final empty socket, bigger than the others.

"Where are the crystals?" Sophia said.

"Shattered," Quinn said. "And the monsters stored in each crystal were released, as was Chaos."

"The monsters are free?" Noah said. Monsters in theory were pretty cool, but Noah wasn't sure he wanted to meet one in real life.

"Free and wreaking havoc on the world, once again," Quinn said.

"Is that why this castle is such a dump?" Ava asked.

Mason smacked her on the arm. "Don't be rude."

"But it is," Ava said. "The walls are collapsing and the roof is about to cave in."

"Oh," Mason said. "So that's not good."

"Not good at all," Quinn said. "And with no magic left in the world, it's even worse than before."

"So what are you going to do about it?" Noah asked.

"Do about it?" Quinn said. "What do you mean? I already did something about it."

"What?" Noah said.

"I thought it was pretty obvious," Quinn said. "That's why the four of you are here. You four are the wizards of tomorrow. You're going to save the world."

CHAPTER 4

O kay, so the story so far was pretty cool, except Quinn was obviously crazy. They were going to save the world? Noah couldn't even save his science grade.

This time, he didn't even try to hold back the laughter. It spilled from his lips and pretty soon Mason joined him. Ava looked like she was ready to press the reset button on this entire adventure. But Sophia . . . her eyes were still locked on Quinn.

"We're going to save the world?" Sophia said.

"No," Noah managed to say once he stopped laughing. "This is a joke. A huge joke. This guy . . . " He motioned at Quinn, " . . . probably isn't even real."

Quinn pressed his fingers together. "Not real? Why would you think that?"

"Because none of this is real," Noah said. "Not you. Not this castle. Not this octagon."

"Octolith," Quinn said. "And I'm sorry if it seems crazy, but we really don't have time to waste arguing about it. You four have been chosen."

"By a game app?" Ava said.

"A game app I designed," Quinn said. "I realized that we didn't have any magic now, so I knew I'd have to find wizards in the past. That's why I created the app. I designed it and uploaded it, just for the four of you to find."

"You wrote the app?" Sophia said. "It's amazing. I mean the graphics aren't that great, but they key and the way we can chat with each other . . . that's really cool."

"I didn't want to spend too much time on the graphics," Quinn said. "All it needed to do was bring you four here."

"You keep saying us four," Mason said. "Why us four? What makes us special?"

Quinn grinned like he'd won the lottery. "Because you four, of everyone else in your time, have magic."

Noah had a moment of truth. When it came right down to it, if it would have ever, even in the slightest bit been possible, been able for him to be some kind of wizard who could run around casting magic spells, he would have been all over that. But no matter how much he might have wanted that to be a reality, it wasn't. It just wasn't.

"I don't have any magic," Noah said.

"I don't either," Ava said.

Noah looked to Sophia who turned to him.

"Look," Sophia said. "I know everything that Quinn is telling us sounds completely crazy. But what if it wasn't? What if it was real? What if everything he's been saying were the truth, and that we really have been brought to the future to use magic and fight monsters? Wouldn't that be the coolest thing in the world? Wouldn't it?"

"Of course it would," Noah said. "But it's not true."

"Oh, I have an idea," Ava said. "How about you prove it to us? Can you do that?"

They all four turned to Quinn.

"Doesn't the Octolith prove it?" Quinn said.

"It's a stone table with some holes in it," Ava said. "That doesn't prove anything."

She had a valid point.

"How do we do this magic?" Mason said. "Are there special words or do we need a wand?"

Quinn shook his head. "Oh, no. Nothing like that."

"Then what?" Mason said.

Quinn shrugged. "Well, in the past, the wizards used stones to channel their power."

"And you have these magic stones?" Ava said.

"Not me," Quinn said. "I don't have the magic. But you four do. And that's why you have the stones."

Noah looked at the back of his hands, wishing he did have some kind of magic stone. But next to him, Sophia exclaimed, "He's right!"

He turned to her. She was staring at her left palm, and the reason why was because there was a white stone embedded right there in the middle of it. She touched it lightly with her other hand, and when she did, her clothes stayed the same in shape and material but shifted colors until they were all red.

Noah flipped his left hand over and was amazed to see that he also had a white stone embedded in the middle of his palm. He touched it, and his clothes shifted to blue. Mason did the same, and his clothes turned green. Finally Ava joined them. She shook her head and flipped her hand over. Her eyes grew wide, and she gently touched it. Her clothes turned purple.

"There you go," Quinn said. "Fire, Water, Earth, and Air. You four are perfect. White means the stones are full of energy, or so I read in the history books. But if you use too much, they turn black and your magic won't work."

"I can't believe this!" Sophia said. "We are in a video game. We are seriously in a video game."

Quinn stood. "Not a video game. This is the real world. And there are monsters that need to be captured or the four of you will have no future to look forward to."

"So we really are the wizards of tomorrow," Noah said, standing also.

Quinn eyes him up and down and then nodded. "I really hope so," he said. "Or else everything is lost."

CHAPTER 5

"This is really cool," Noah said. "But I'm already going to be in so much trouble at home. Can we come back tomorrow and save the day?" He knew it sounded completely lame, but he was already so far over his ten minutes until folding laundry time that he was probably going to have to spend his entire spring break doing chores, not just the start of it.

"Your mom will understand," Sophia said. "When you explain to her that you need to save the world, everything will be totally cool."

"Right," Noah said. "And she's just going to believe it."

"She will when you do magic," Mason said.

"About that," Quinn said. "The stones in your hands can't travel back into the past with you. They stay here in the future because they're technology that was created in the future. But the good news is that since we are in the future, no time will have passed once you return."

"And we can return whenever we want?" Ava said. She still had a skeptical look on her face, like she mostly expected this to be make-believe.

"Yeah, and that," Quinn said. "You can only return once the monster has been recaptured."

"And what if the monster isn't recaptured?" Ava said. "Or what if we die trying to capture it?"

Quinn put a finger to his lips. "That would be most unfortunate."

"Unfortunate," Noah said. "That sounds so reassuring."

But Quinn only said, "The only thing reassuring about our world right now is that fact that the four of you are here. You're basically our only hope."

"You guys are in serious trouble," Mason said.

"Fine, so how do we capture this monster?" Sophia said. Even if it wasn't a video game, it was at least still kind of like one. Capture the monster and the level would be done.

"Oh, it's really very simple," Quinn said. "All you have to do is get a new crystal for the Octolith from the monkeys, and then use that crystal to trap the monster."

Noah stared at him like he'd lost his mind. "You realize that gives us no information at all."

"Yeah, like what monkeys? What crystal? Where is the monster?" Ava said.

Quinn looked at them like they'd all gone crazy. "That's why the four of you are here. You're the wizards. You have to figure that out."

Noah was about to ask Quinn something else, except he never got the chance. Quinn vanished.

"Oh, that's just perfect," Ava said. "He tells us exactly what we don't need to know, and then he vanishes."

Noah couldn't disagree. After Quinn's explanation of whatever was going on, he had more questions than answers. They were in the future? For real? And they'd been transported through some sort of video game app? If it was really true, then it was the coolest thing he'd ever heard. And the freakiest.

"Where'd he go?" Sophia said. Her eyes were huge, and Noah couldn't tell whether she was upset that her video game hero had vanished or excited about the fact that she now got to take the lead. She ran over to the seat where Quinn had been only seconds before.

"Gone," Mason said. He placed a hand on Ava's shoulder, almost like he was trying to calm her through some kind of twin link.

"Yeah, great, gone," Ava said. "So now we do what? Just sit here and wait for some monster to come eat us?"

"You think the monsters eat people?" Noah said.

Ava spun on him. "Monsters always eat people. Don't you ever read stories?"

Noah let out a small laugh. "Those are book monsters. Not real monsters."

"And you think they're different?" Ava said.

Up until this entire moment, Noah had never actually thought one way or the other about it because monsters weren't real. Except now, apparently, monsters were real. And were destroying the world. Again.

Noah shook his head. "Maybe?"

"It doesn't matter," Sophia said. "What does matter is we have to do what Quinn said."

"What?" Ava said. "Find some monkeys? What monkeys?"

Sophia shrugged. "Monkeys."

Something nagged at the back of Noah's mind, but he couldn't remember what. But he remembered something his mom had said about how if you squeeze your hand into a fist, it helps you remember. So he squeezed his right fingers tight, and then it came back to him.

"The tapestry," he said, snapping his eyes open. He hadn't even realized that he'd closed them.

"What about the tapestry?" Mason said.

"It's stupid," Ava said. "That's what."

"No!" Noah said. "It had monkeys on it. When we came into this room."

He didn't wait for the three of them to figure out what he was talking about. Instead, he dashed back out the door they'd come from, back into the room with the fireplace. Sophia immediately followed him, but Ava dragged her feet. It was only her twin, Mason, pulling on her arm that got her back into the fireplace room. Once they were all there, Noah dropped the giant tapestry back into place, covering the door opening.

"This," Noah said, letting the tapestry fall.

There it was. He knew he'd seen the monkeys. Because there on the tapestry were three monkeys sitting on a rock by a river. One had its hands over its eyes. One had its hands over its ears. And one had its hands over its mouth.

"I know these monkeys," Mason said. "Remember, Ava?"

"Remember what?" Ava said.

"The little monkey statues Dad has sitting on his desk. He says they're Japanese and that they mean 'See no evil. Hear no evil. Speak no evil.' They're kind of reddish."

"Maybe," Ava says.

Sophia stepped forward and ran her hand over the tapestry. "Do you think we ask the tapestry where the crystal we need is? Or where the monster is?"

Noah had no clue, but it sounded like as good an idea as any. He stepped forward next to her.

"Great monkeys, tell us where the magic crystal to trap the monster is." He felt kind of stupid saying it, but having never talked to magical monkeys before, he wasn't sure what else to say. Behind him, he heard Mason laugh.

Of course nothing happened. The monkeys in the tapestry weren't alive and as a result didn't move.

"I don't think that's it," Sophia said. "We need to find this rock. Find this river."

"You mean go outside?" Noah said. Outside was where the man-eating monsters were, at least according to Quinn.

"Are you scared?" Mason said, and something in the way he said it made Noah want to prove to him that he wasn't scared at all.

"Of course I'm not scared," Noah said.

"We need a map," Sophia said. "You always need a map in video games."

"This isn't a video game," Ava said.

Sophia put her hands on her hips and looked right at Ava. "No, but it's like a video game, and maybe that's what we need to do. Pretend it's a video game."

Ava opened her mouth like she was going to argue with Sophia but then shut it. That seemed like as much agreement as they were all going to get right now.

"We need to find the way out of this castle," Mason said, glancing around the room. There was the fireplace, the tapestry hiding the room with the Octolith, the stairway Noah had come down from when he first arrived here, and then there was another opening, a hallway on one of the opposite walls.

"What's down there?" Noah said.

But Ava had already started toward it, with Mason following right behind her. Noah looked to Sophia who shrugged. So be it. Down the dark hallway they went.

The hallway led them on one path, with no other doors or openings. And unlike the main room of the castle they'd been in earlier which had fallen to disrepair, every stone in the walls and ceiling was firmly in place, almost like it had been protected somehow.

Protected from the monsters' attack, Noah thought.

He couldn't believe how easily the thought came to him. He wasn't even sure if this whole world was real. And monsters. But whatever. He trudged forward.

"I see a light ahead," Sophia said. She had made her way up front, so she was next to Ava, leaving Noah and Mason trailing along behind them.

"It's got to be the outside," Ava said, and sure enough, the light began to grow until there was no doubt about it. An opening lay ahead.

Noah's stomach tightened. "Maybe we shouldn't go outside," he said.

"We have to go outside," Sophia said. "We have to find the monster."

That was exactly what Noah was afraid of.

"Okay, I get that," Noah said. "But maybe before we just step out into the monster infested world, we should try to use whatever magic Quinn claims we have." He held up his left hand and stared at the white stone.

Ava spun around to face him. "Go ahead and try." She placed her hands on her hips and waited.

So Noah did just that. He closed his fist and he thought magical thoughts, whatever those were.

Nothing happened.

Of course he had no idea what he was supposed to do. Would it have been too much to ask for there to be some kind of instruction manual?

"You guys try," Noah said, because maybe he just didn't have his magical powers yet. Maybe they needed to develop over time.

Sophia squeezed her hand shut, the same way he had. Again, nothing happened. Ava acted like it was a huge burden, sighing deeply, but then she did the same. She had no better luck than the two of them.

Mason held his hand wide open, like he was casting out a light beam from the white stone.

"Watch me do magic!" he said in a deep booming voice like he was trying to be a stage magician.

Underneath them, the entire ground shook.

CHAPTER 7

"You did it!" Sophia shouted. She jumped up, and Noah wasn't sure whether it was from pure excitement or from the ground shaking.

"That was a coincidence," Ava said, but her normally super confident voice was filled with doubt.

"Do it again," Noah said. He wanted to believe that it was magic, and that they really were wizards, but he also needed proof.

"Do you think I need to say the words again?" Mason said.

Ava smacked him on the shoulder. "Just do it again."

So Mason held his hand out again. This time he didn't say anything. Only focused his eyes on the ground.

It started out slow, like a small tremor, but then it full-on shook once again, making Noah lose his balance for a second.

"You're doing magic!" Sophia said. "You really are."

She was completely right. Once might have been a coincidence. But twice? That was pretty hard to deny.

Mason looked to Ava. Her mouth hung open and her eyes were wide.

"What did you do?" she said, staring at the white stone in her hand.

Mason almost looked like he didn't believe it himself. "I just thought about it. I thought magical thoughts."

"What are magical thoughts?" Ava said.

He shrugged. "I don't know. They're just magical thoughts."

Noah held his hand out like Mason had done, and tried all the magical thoughts that he could, but nothing happened. And since he didn't know what to expect, it made it that much harder.

"You must be the Earth wizard," Sophia said, hurrying over to stand by Mason. "That's really cool."

"Yeah, I guess so," Mason said.

A weird wave of jealousy ran though Noah, but he quickly shoved it away. Still, so what if Mason was some kind of Earth wizard? Whatever.

"But look at the stone," Sophia said. "It's gray."

Mason flipped his hand over so they all could see. Sure enough, the stone that had been white only seconds before was more of a dingy gray now.

"You think it will recharge?" Mason said, and worry filled his voice.

"I'm sure of it," Sophia said. "Quinn said that it just takes time."

"I'm going outside," Noah said, stepping past Sophia and Mason. He was only about twenty steps away from the doorway, and he covered the distance, not looking back. Still, he hoped the others were following him.

The opening was bright white, but besides that, he couldn't see anything. It was like a white curtain had been hung over the opening. Noah took a deep breath and stepped through.

He had no idea what he was expecting, but whatever it was, it was not this. He was in a city, with paved streets and apartments and stores and office buildings. But instead of a nice shiny city, the entire place looked like the end of the world had come. The tops had been ripped off of skyscrapers. Windows of apartments had been torn away from the building, collapsing the rest of the structure around them. Huge chunks had been ripped from the streets and tossed into piles, leaving giant holes in the ground. And to make matters even worse, the bright white light from the tunnel had been an illusion. The sky outside was gray and it was raining.

"This is not good," Ava said, coming up beside Noah.

He never would have admitted it, but after seeing this place, it was nice to know that he wasn't out here alone. Gray clouds filled the sky, moving so quickly that even if there had been shapes, they changed too fast to pretend they were animals or cotton candy or anything fun like that.

"You think the monsters did all this?" he asked.

"I guess," Ava said. She squeezed her left fist shut over the stone.

"Is that a sign?" Sophia said. She and Mason came out of the castle opening together.

"Where?" Noah said.

"Over there." Sophia pointed about a block away, near a giant pile of torn down building material.

Noah squinted so he could see better. Sure enough, it did look like something was over there. He started

44

walking toward it, stepping over the torn ground until he reached it.

"It's a map," Sophia said, coming up next to him.

"Of this place?" Mason said.

"Looks like it." Sophia pointed at the map. Each place she touched lit up. "See, here's the castle. And here's where we just walked—"

"Do you see the rocks with the monkeys?" Noah said. He scanned the map also. At the top of it, there were the words ULTIMATE TRAVEL AGENT, like it was an advertisement for a travel agency that had been destroyed by monsters, just like everything else in this world. But instead of looking all cool with pictures and stuff like that, it was more like one of those maps that he'd seen in shopping malls, with different colored blocks for all the different stores and levels. There was a blue box that was clearly labeled OCTOLITH CASTLE, and a yellow star right nearby that said YOU ARE HERE.

"This must be water," Mason said, touching a blue line that ran along the right side of the map.

The second his finger touched the map, it lit up, drawing a red line from where they were to the place that he'd pushed. That's when Noah felt his cell phone vibrate in his pocket. He pulled it out and turned it on.

And there, on the screen was the exact same map that was in front of them, only pocket sized.

"It's part of the app," Sophia said, pulling her phone out also. "Let's follow it."

And because nobody could think of a single reason not to, they started walking.

Noah split his attention between watching their progress on the map app on his phone and scanning the nearby area to make sure a monster didn't jump out and eat them.

"This is part of the *Wizards of Tomorrow* app," Sophia said, almost bouncing up and down from excitement. "And you see these four dots that are different colors . . . those are us. I'm red, like my clothes."

It was true. They could each be seen on the screen.

"Why do cell phones still work here?" Ava said. "If we really are five hundred years in the future, doesn't it seem like . . . oh I don't know . . . like maybe Sprint and AT&T aren't in business anymore?"

"Maybe there's some other kind of cell service," Mason said. He stared at the gray stone in his hand, like he was hoping he could will it to somehow turn white again instantly.

"Whatever it is, there's definitely water," Noah said. "I can smell it."

The sky was still gray, but the scent in the air shifted, like fresh water was nearby. It was way different than the city. Back there everything had smelled like dust and decay. Had a bunch of people died back in the city or were they in hiding? And if they were in hiding, did they really think he and his friends would save the day? Noah wasn't sure he wanted the world to depend on his ability to capture a monster, seeing as how he'd never done it before.

"You can smell the water?" Ava said. "I don't smell water."

Noah sniffed the air again. There was no doubting it. He could smell the cool freshness and fish and algae and other things living in the river ahead. Yes, it was a river. He was sure of it. He closed his eyes, trying to get a better picture of it, and there was no mistaking it. He could almost see it in his mind.

"There are rocks. And right nearby a little waterfall," Noah said.

Ava looked like she didn't believe a word that was coming out of his mouth, but every step they got closer, he was sure of it. It was almost like he could feel the water running through him.

That's why, when they scrambled through the remains of a brick wall that must have been the city border, he wasn't surprised at what he saw. It looked exactly like it did in his mind.

Ava said, "You're right. How are you right?"

He opened his mouth, as if looking for the answer. "I . . ." He couldn't put it into words. He had just known.

"Noah, you're holding your hand out," Sophia said.

He looked down, realizing that she was right. He held his left hand in front of him, like some kind of seeing device. When he touched the stone, it felt warm.

"You're the water wizard," Sophia said. "That has to be it."

"What? Because he heard water?" Mason said. "That doesn't prove anything."

It was like Mason didn't want anyone else to have magic.

"I didn't hear it," Noah said. "I felt it. And if you can say you had magical thoughts, then I can say that I felt water."

He wasn't trying to argue with Mason, but it only made sense that they should each have magic. That's why Quinn had brought them here.

"I think it's really cool," Sophia said.

Noah smiled, but Mason scowled.

"You guys see those rocks?" Ava said, pointing off to the left, down the river.

They turned to look. She was right. Way off in the distance was a huge rock surrounded by a bunch of other smaller ones.

It didn't take them long to reach the rocks. And when they got there, sitting on top of the biggest rock which was at least twenty feet in the air, were three monkeys.

CHAPTER 8

"It's just like on the tapestry," Noah said, pointing up at the monkeys. One sat covering its eyes, one covering its ears, and one covering its mouth.

If the monkeys noticed them, they didn't react. They only sat there staring off into the distance, as if they were contemplating the deeper meaning of life.

"Hey you!" Ava called up, cupping her hands around her mouth so her voice would carry farther.

The monkeys didn't move.

"You!" she said. "Monkeys on the rock!"

Nothing.

"You smell bad!" Ava hollered.

This finally worked. The monkey covering its eyes swiveled its head around. "Who said that?"

"I said that," Ava said, sticking her hands on her hips like she was daring the monkey to complain about it.

"Who?" the monkey said. "You sound like a squirmy little brat, but I can't see you."

"That's because you're covering your eyes," Mason said.

"I am? Oh, right, I am," he said, but he still didn't uncover his eyes.

"What?" the monkey next to him, covering his ears, said.

"Some little brat told us that we smell bad," Mr. No-Eyes said. Noah figured that was as good a nickname as any.

"What?" Mr. No-Ears said.

"I said that some little brat told us we smell bad," Mr. No-Eyes said.

"Mmrmrmrmrmrmr," the monkey covering his mouth said.

"What?" both Mr. No-Eyes and Mr. No-Ears said.

"This is ridiculous," Ava said. "If you all would just uncover your eyes, ears, and mouth this would be so much easier."

"See, that's the brat I'm talking about," Mr. No-Eyes said. "She says we smell bad."

"Mmmrmrmrmmr," Mr. No-Mouth said.

"We need a crystal," Sophia finally said. "Quinn told us you three monkeys had it."

"Who's that?" Mr. No-Eyes said. "Another little brat?"

"There are four of us," Sophia said. If she was bothered by the little brat comment, she didn't let on.

"Four brats?" Mr. No-Eyes said. "Where are you?"

Mr. No-Mouth kept one hand over his mouth but pointed at them with his other hand and mumbled something that Noah thought was probably along the line of, 'There they are.' Not that it would help. Mr. No-Eyes couldn't see where he was pointing, and Mr. No-Ears couldn't hear anything.

"Look," Noah said, deciding that they had to get past these completely unhelpful introductions. "We came for a crystal. Some guy named Quinn set us."

"Quinn," Mr. No-Eyes said. "Never heard of him."

But Mr. No-Mouth started mumbling again and bounced up and down on his feet, like maybe he didn't quite agree.

"Do you have the crystal?" Noah said. "We need to trap the . . . some monster." He realized that he had no idea what kind of monster they were trying to trap.

"Little brats like you?" Mr. No-Eyes said. "How are little brats like you going to trap a monster?"

"What are they saying?" Mr. No-Ears said.

"You should learn to read lips," Mason called out. "Then you'd be able to understand us."

"He could understand us if he uncovered his ears," Ava said.

"I asked them why they think they can trap a monster," Mr. No-Eyes said to Mr. No-Ears.

"What?" Mr. No-Ears said.

This was ridiculous. Noah finally said, "We're wizards."

All three monkeys stopped bouncing around and looked at him. Well, Mr. No-Eyes looked in his direction but still kept his eyes covered.

"What did they say?" Mr. No-Ears said.

Mr. No-Eyes set his mouth in a thin line. "They say that they're wizards."

"What?" Mr. No-Ears said.

"Wizards," Mr. No-Eyes said. "But they can't be. There are no more wizards. All the wizards are gone."

"We're Wizards of Tomorrow," Sophia said. "We came from the past."

"The past?" Mr. No-Eyes said. He turned to the other two monkeys, like he hoped somehow they'd magically be able to communicate with him. But with their self-imposed limitations, that was pretty much impossible.

"Yes, the past," Mason said.

"What part of the past?" Mr. No-Eyes said.

Noah couldn't take it anymore. He held his left hand out in frustration and squeezed his eyes shut. These monkeys had to be the most annoying monkeys in the entire world, past or present.

He felt a wave of energy move through him, from the white stone in his hand out through every part of his body. And the next thing he heard was a giant splash of water.

Noah opened his eyes.

The monkeys were sopping wet. Water dripped from them and poured down the rocks they sat on.

"You did that!" Sophia said.

"Did what?" Noah asked. He'd had his eyes closed and hadn't seen anything.

"You pulled water up from the river and dumped it on the monkeys."

"You did that?" Mr. No-Eyes said. He shook his head and water went flying everywhere.

Noah knew he did it. He felt it inside.

"I told you that we're wizards," Noah said. "So do you have a crystal for us to capture the monster or not?"

Mr. No-Mouth mumbled something, but Mr. No-Ears seemed to understand because he kept nodding his head. Then he turned to Mr. No-Eyes and started rattling off some kind of monkey language that Noah couldn't understand. Finally Mr. No-Eyes turned back in their direction even though he couldn't see them.

"So we're wondering," Mr. No-Eyes said. "What monster are you trying to catch?"

"We don't know," Mason said.

"Would it perhaps be the Manticore?" Mr. No-Eyes said.

"Maybe," Mason said. "Why?"

"He's been causing trouble in a town nearby," Mr. No-Eyes said.

Noah had no idea if that was the monster they were after, but he also wanted the monkeys to think the four of them knew what they were doing. "It is the Manticore," Noah said.

"Manticore," Mr. No-Eyes said, and then a whole bunch more monkey jibberish got passed between the three monkeys.

Sophia leaned over and whispered to Noah, "That was really cool with the water."

"Thanks," Noah said, and he felt his face get really hot, which was weird. He talked to Sophia all the time. She never made his stomach feel all funny.

Finally all three monkeys looked in their direction. "We have this crystal," Mr. No-Eyes finally said. "But there's one problem."

"What?" Ava said.

He used his head to motion at Mr. No-Mouth. "It's in his mouth."

Mr. No-Mouth nodded his head, all the while keeping his hand over his mouth.

"And that's a problem why?" Ava said.

Mr. No-Mouth mumbled something, and Mr. No-Eyes said, "Because he's covering it."

"So he can just uncover it," Ava said.

"And why is it in his mouth anyway?" Mason said.

"He can't uncover it," Mr. Eyes said. "And it's in his mouth because he put it in there."

This was the craziest conversation Noah had ever had. "I have an idea," Noah said. "How about I climb up there and pull his hand off his mouth and he spits it out?"

The monkeys seemed to consider this.

"That might work," Mr. No-Eyes said.

But before he could start climbing, Ava scrambled up the rock. She moved so fast, it was almost like the wind was pushing her upward. Before he knew it, she was at the top, next to Mr. No-Mouth.

Ava put one hand on Mr. No-Mouth's hand and the other on his forehead and then yanked his hand off his mouth. The second his mouth was uncovered, he spit out a blue crystal. It flew through the air, flipping end over end until it landed at Sophia's feet. She bent down and picked it up.

"Yuck! It's covered with monkey drool," Sophia said.

"We got it!" Mason said, giving Sophia a high five.

Ava scurried back down the rocks, joining them at the bottom.

"Now we just have to find the Manticore," Noah said.

On cue, from off in the distance, a piercing scream filled the air.

CHAPTER 9

"Wait!" Mr. No-Mouth said. "There are three things you need to know about the Manticore."

Noah had to double check to make sure it was him talking since all he'd done so far was mumble. But sure enough, Mr. No-Mouth still had his mouth uncovered and was apparently going to tell them about the monster.

"What things?" Ava said.

The other two monkeys jumped up and down while Mr. No-Mouth spoke.

"It shoots poisonous spikes from its tail," Mr. No-Mouth said. "Which looks like the tail of a scorpion but is like a thousand times bigger."

"Wonderful," Mason said. "What else?"

"It had claws like a lion that can tear you to shreds," Mr. No-Mouth said. He swiped out a hand like he was clawing the air.

"Okay, that's two," Mason said. "What's the third thing?"

"Right," Mr. No-Mouth said. "It has three rows of teeth that it uses to devour its victims. Rumor has it that the teeth cut right through bone, making it so that it leaves nothing behind."

"Isn't that hard on digestion?" Ava said.

Noah almost laughed. Almost, except the image of a monster with three rows of teeth made him shudder instead.

Mr. No-Mouth didn't waste any time. His hand flew back over his mouth, covering it.

"Well, thanks for all that," Ava said.

She held her hand out, palm up, and Noah swore that she almost levitated over the ground.

"Are you flying?" he asked.

She looked down, then looked to the stone in her hand. "Maybe." The stone was grayish but wasn't getting any darker.

He pressed on her shoulder, and her feet touched the ground and then she bounced back up. "You are. You can fly."

"I don't think I'd call that flying," Mason said. "More like hovering."

Ava crossed her arms and started at Mason.

"Hovering is still pretty cool," Sophia said.

Just then, they heard another scream.

"We need to go," Noah said. If the Manticore really could eat people, and if they could help, then they had to at least try.

"Oh, wait!" Mr. No-Eyes said. "Did he tell you about the butterflies?"

"Butterflies?"

Mr. No-Eyes looked to Mr. No-Mouth who started mumbling something excitedly.

"What's he saying?" Ava said.

Mr. No-Eyes just shook his head. "I hope it doesn't matter."

They left the monkeys there on the rocks and started in the direction of the scream.

"So Ava can fly," Sophia said.

"Hover," Mason corrected.

"Ava can hover," Sophia said. "Mason can make the ground shake. Noah can move water. What about me? What can I do?"

She held her left hand out, but if she was doing something magical, Noah couldn't tell what it was.

"It's gotta be fire," Ava said. "That's the only element left."

"And nothing's happening," Sophia said. "That's just great."

Noah tried to think of something to say to make her feel better, but nothing came to mind.

Even though Quinn told them that no time would pass in the past, Noah still couldn't help worrying about the fact that with each step they took it got darker. Which meant it was also longer away from home. What if time really did pass? His mom was going to freak out. But those worries went away when he tripped on something in the path and almost landed on his face.

"I can't see a thing," Noah said. His hands were covered in dirt, and he wiped them on his pants.

"Me either," Sophia said. Noah couldn't see her face, but her voice sounded disappointed. "But we have to be close. Those have to be monster screams."

"I hear them, too," Ava said. "But trying to attack it in the pitch black is a horrible idea. It probably has some special abilities where it can see in the dark."

Sophia blew out a breath. "But we have to get there. We have to catch it."

"Tomorrow," Mason said, and he plunked down on the ground, right there in the middle of the path they were walking on.

Ava sat down next to him, pulling her knees up to her chest.

Noah looked in Sophia's direction. "I'm sorry, Sophia. But I can't see a thing. We have to stop. Otherwise the Manticore is going to eat us."

He was about to sit down, but Sophia said, "No. We can't stop."

And she held her left hand out, palm up.

The air in front of her erupted in fire.

Resting on her left hand was a big brilliant fire ball, with flames curling all around.

"That is awesome!" Mason said, jumping up from the ground. "You made fire!"

"Yeah, pretty cool," Ava said.

"And now we don't have to stop," Sophia said. "This more than lights up our path."

She was completely right. Light emanated from the fire ball. Noah saw the very tree root that he tripped over.

"I knew you'd be fire," Noah said to Sophia once they started walking again.

"It's really cool, Noah," Sophia said. "It doesn't burn at all."

Noah decided against reaching out and touching it. Since he wasn't a fire wizard, it would almost certainly burn him. Just the heat coming off it warmed his skin.

The walked for another half hour until finally, as the light stretched out, they saw the remains of a neighborhood in front of them.

"You think the monsters did this?" Mason said, motioning at the houses. Like the city they'd started in, all the houses were falling apart.

"I guess so," Noah said. "Do you think we're too late?"

"Too late for what?" Ava said. "The monsters are already out. The whole reason we're here is because it's too late. All we can do is try to make things better."

She made complete sense. They couldn't fix what had happened. They could only prevent more harm from happening in the future.

"You see that?" Noah said, pointing over to a nearby house. Most of the roof was caved in, and from the remains was the flickering light of a campfire.

"People live here," Sophia said. "The Manticore didn't eat them all."

"Do you think it ate any of them?" Noah said. He couldn't get past the idea of a monster crunching through bone. The sound alone made him want to throw up.

"Of course it ate people," Ava said. "Are you forgetting the part where Quinn said that the monsters destroyed the world and that what humans were left tried to rebuild? That means a lot of humans weren't left. Unless there's something I'm missing."

Noah wished there was something she was missing, but this wasn't a video game. People had died. And they had to stop more people from dying.

"How do we find the monster?" Mason said.

"Well, I guess we ask her," Sophia said.

They turned in the direction of the firelight. Walking toward them was a woman. She was holding something in her hands, and she didn't look happy at all.

CHAPTER 10

"Don't attack her!" Sophia said, still holding the fire ball.

Noah hadn't planned on attacking her, but now that Sophia mentioned it, what if the woman thought they were the monster and was going to attack them?

"We're here to help!" Sophia called out.

The woman stopped and with the firelight, Noah could see the look of hope that stretched onto her face.

"You can help?" the woman said.

"Yeah, we can help," Mason said, stepping forward. "We're wizards."

"Wizards?" the woman said. "Then you came to stop the Manticore?"

Noah really hoped that they'd be able to. This woman looked like she was ready to run up and hug them, and they hadn't done anything yet.

"Yeah, we came to stop the Manticore," Ava said. "Have you seen it? Can you tell us where it is?"

The woman looked around in the darkness. "You shouldn't attack at night. Come back to my house. I'll make you dinner and tell you what I know."

At the word dinner, Noah's stomach grumbled. He looked to Sophia who shrugged. And then they followed the woman back to one of the nearby houses. It was only once they were inside and the light bounced around the room, lighting it up, that Noah could see what was wrapped in a blanket in her arms.

"You have a pig," Noah said. Cradled in the woman's arms like a baby was a brownish pink pig that was no bigger than his dog, Xena, back home.

The woman hugged the pig close and kissed its head. Noah wasn't sure whether that was sanitary, but he didn't say anything.

"He's the last one left," the woman said. "The Manticore ate the others."

"It ate your pigs?" Mason said.

Tears crept into the woman's eyes. "They were like my babies. And it ate all but one. Little Homer is all I have left."

Homer looked as happy to be alive as the woman was. He made cute little pig noises and squirmed as she tickled him.

"I forgot to introduce myself," the woman said, setting the pig on the ground near them. She pulled a gate across the door so Homer the pig couldn't run away. "I'm Jessie. And Homer is my baby. It's just the two of us now."

Noah didn't know what else to do, so he introduced himself, and Sophia, Mason, and Ava did the same.

Then Jessie said, "I was making a cake for dinner. Does that sound okay?"

That sounded perfect to Noah. Him mom never let him eat cake before his real dinner. Maybe he'd just stay here in the future forever and eat cake all the time. Except then Jessie put the cake in front of them.

It was brown and lumpy and the only reason it could be considered a cake was because it was mostly in the shape of a circle. Other than that, it was the most disgusting-looking thing Noah had ever seen. He glanced sideways to Sophia.

"Ooh, what's in it?" Sophia asked.

Jessie only shook her head. "You don't want to know."

Noah did his best to pick at it and not be rude while Jessie told them about the Manticore.

"It showed up probably six months ago," Jessie said. "We'd only ever heard rumors about the monsters. We'd always assumed they were trapped for good. The first night, it ate five cows. Five! I couldn't imagine how one monster could eat so many cows, so I snuck out and spied on it. It's at least twenty feet tall at the shoulders.

Its head looks like a lion. Its tail has sharp spikes. And the horrible noise it makes sounds just like a human scream. I think that's so people will think someone is in trouble, and they'll go looking to try to help."

"Has it eaten any people yet?" Mason asked.

"Only Crazy Joe," Jessie said. "Or at least we think it ate him. We haven't seen him in a couple months."

Noah wanted to ask who Crazy Joe was, but he didn't want to draw attention to himself because he still hadn't made very good progress with the cake meal.

"Do you know how to find the monster?" Sophia asked.

"Find it?" Jessie said. "Why do you want to find it?"

Ava put her hands on her hips. Unlike Noah, she'd eaten her entire portion of cake. He subtly pushed his in her direction.

"We want to find it because like we said, we're wizards and we're going to trap it," Ava said.

"You really are wizards?" Jessie said. "Can you do magic?"

Ava seemed to have had enough. "Yes, we can do magic," she said, and she held out her hand. Wind whipped through the house, making the flames of the fire dance and the ash from the fire pit blow around. Homer the pig whimpered and hid under Jessie's legs.

"That's magic," Ava said.

"Oooh," Jessie said. "You really are wizards."

Noah was glad that he hadn't had to prove it. It had felt so natural when he'd doused the monkeys, but now he wasn't sure if he could do it again.

"So where's the Manticore?" Noah said.

"If I tell you, you have to wait until morning. He hunts at night," Jessie said.

That suited Noah just fine.

"Deal," Mason said.

"He lives on an island," Jessie said. "In the middle of the lake, center of town. It used to be one of those decorative lakes, with a fountain and people fishing in boats. But now no one goes near it."

No one except them, Noah though. Because tomorrow that was going to be exactly what they would do. They would go to the lake and find the Manticore.

Noah hardly slept at all that night. He kept hearing screams fill the air, as if the Manticore was trying to draw them toward it. Noah only clamped his hands over his ears, like he was the Hear-no-evil monkey, Mr. No-Ears. If only that would be enough. Before he knew it, the sky lightened and the sun burst through the gaping holes in the roof of the house.

"Thanks for the cake," Ava said.

"Do you want some for the road?" Jessie said, reaching for the pan which still sat on the counter.

"No, that's okay," Noah said. Maybe there would be an apple tree along the way. Or a lemon tree. Raw lemons would be better than the mush cake.

"I hope the Manticore doesn't eat you," Jessie said, and then she shooed them out the door, like she didn't want to have anything to do with the monsters.

"Can you tell where the lake is?" Mason asked Noah.

Noah held his hand out and closed his eyes. It seemed to help him focus better. He turned around in a circle. He could feel the water in the air. He could hear the lapping of the water against the shore. It was like if he reached out, he could touch it, even though it wasn't anywhere nearby.

"That way," Noah said, opening his eyes and nodding in the direction he was facing.

"You sure?" Ava said.

Noah narrowed his eyes at her. "I'm sure. I'm a water wizard, remember?"

"Yeah, I remember," she said. "But you're still learning."

"So are you," Noah said.

"Let's go check it out," Sophia said, starting in that direction.

Mason hurried and caught up with her, leaving Noah to walk next to Ava. They didn't talk as they walked. She always seemed like she had to prove something, and Noah didn't want to worry about that. Right now, they needed to worry about the Manticore.

They walked for a good fifteen minutes before they finally came to the lake. It appeared out of nowhere, behind a giant clump of trees. The good news was that it was a lake with an island in the middle, just like Jessie had said. The bad news was that it was a really big lake, like huge, and the island was way far away, in the middle.

"We're going to need a boat," Mason said.

CHAPTER 11

Noah looked around. There were at least a hundred boats scattered around the shore, maybe left over from the fishing days, but they were all in pieces.

"I don't think any of these boats will work," Noah said.

"So what are we supposed to do?" Mason said. "Fly across?"

"Maybe," Ava said, and she lifted up into the air, hovering a foot off the ground.

"That is so cool," Sophia said.

"Can you make all of us hover?" Noah asked. If she could, they wouldn't need a boat.

Ava seemed to concentrate for a moment while holding her hand. She stared right at him.

Nothing happened except the white stone grew darker.

"I don't think so," Ava said. "I think it will use up all my magic if I try."

Maybe she just didn't know enough about magic yet, Noah thought. But he didn't want to say that and have Ava get all defensive.

Noah walked over to a nearby boat. Two of the sides had fallen completely off, but the bottom and the two other sides were mostly intact. He started pulling it toward the water.

"You realize that boat will sink," Mason said.

"Yeah, true," Noah said. "But I'm wondering. If use my magic to keep water from getting on it maybe it'll be enough to get us across."

"That might work," Mason said, and he helped Noah pull it until it rested just at the edge of the water.

Noah held out his left hand, and Mason pushed the boat out into the water. Noah thought about the water, about keeping it away from the edges of the boat.

It worked!

The water lapped right at the edges of the bottom of the boat, but didn't pour over into it.

"It's working!" Sophia said, and without waiting for the others, she jumped on board . . . a little too hard. Water sloshed over, but Noah was prepared. He pushed it away. Next Mason stepped on board, and finally Noah himself. Ava lifted up into the air and floated next to the boat. There was only one problem.

"It's not moving," Mason said.

"Yeah, I realize that," Noah said.

"Can you make the water move?" Sophia asked.

So Noah tried, pushing his thoughts toward the water under the boat, and moving it in the direction of the island. The boat started moving.

But sweat began to break out on his forehead and drip down his face and the white stone in his palm was dark gray. This was hard work. And the more he thought about how hard it was, the harder it got.

"There's water coming over the side," Sophia said. "We're going to sink."

The water was black and smelled like a toilet. Falling into it was not going to be pleasant.

"Scoop the water out," Noah said, and he tried to keep the water away. They were getting closer to the island, but still had a ways to go. The stone kept getting darker. If it turned completely black, they'd be in real trouble.

"There's too much," Mason said.

That's when every bit of magical power Noah felt left him, slipping out like all the air leaving his lungs. Water poured over the sides of the boat, and soon they were ankle deep in water. Then it reached their knees, and before anyone could do anything, the three of them fell into the water, going under.

Noah bobbed his head above the water. The shore wasn't too far away.

"We have to swim," he called, and they started toward the shore. That's when the water started to ripple, as if some giant creature who lived underneath it had smelled them and was coming to devour them.

"Hurry!" Ava said, floating in the air around them. She stayed right near Mason who was swimming as fast as he could.

But whatever was in the water was faster. It was getting closer with every second that went by.

"We're not going to make it," Mason said.

Just as the words left his mouth, an enormous head lifted up out of the water and opened its gaping mouth. It was like a giant swimming dinosaur fish, and it was going to eat them.

CHAPTER 12

"Το you don't!" Ava screamed, and a huge burst of wind hit the creature in the head. It flew backward. Noah, Mason, and Sophia took that as their opportunity and swam the final distance to the island before the fish creature could come back. They scrambled up on the sandy shore and collapsed. Ava sank to the ground next to them, and lay flat on her back. She flipped her hand over. The stone in her palm was black, just like Noah's.

"It worked," she said, and she closed her eyes.

"That was amazing," Noah said. "You saved us."

"Yeah," Ava said. "And don't forget it. You guys owe me. You all owe me."

"Enough," Mason said, dusting the sand off his clothes. And then a giant clump of sand lifted up from the ground and poured over the top of Ava's head.

"Hey!" she said, sitting up.

"I just don't want you to think you're the only one with special powers," Mason said.

Then the ground rumbled.

Sophia spun to look at Mason. "Please tell me that you did that," she said.

Mason slowly shook his head. "It wasn't me."

"Then that means—" Noah started.

A scream pierced the air.

"That means it's the Manticore," Sophia said.

They all four turned to look in the direction the scream had come from, but all they could see were trees. Except the trees were moving, swaying back and forth as if something huge was pushing them around and playing with them.

"Are we ready for this?" Noah asked.

Ava crossed her arms. "Do we have a choice?"

There was another scream, closer this time. It made goosebumps explode on Noah's skin.

"I don't think so," Mason said.

"It'll be easy," Sophia said. "We'll just capture the monster with the blue crystal." But even she didn't sound entirely convinced.

"You still have the crystal, right?" Ava said.

Sophia nodded and pulled it from her pocket.

The trees rustled again, and the ground rumbled.

"Easy you think?" Noah said.

"Maybe," Sophia said.

There was a final rustling in the trees, and then they gaped apart.

The Manticore shoved itself through the opening in the trees. It spotted them, lifted its lion's head, and screamed, just like a person in horrible pain. Horrible pain that the four of them would be in if this didn't work. They would be like Jessie's pigs, eaten by the monster.

"Maybe not easy," Sophia said, and she held the blue crystal aloft.

Noah wasn't sure how it was supposed to work. Did it just suck in the monster? Did they have to get close to it? Quinn hadn't told them anything.

The Manticore advanced on them, taking one booming step after the other. If it was affected by the crystal, Noah couldn't tell. It stopped about twenty feet away and tossed its giant head around, roaring and screaming. Mason clamped his hands over his ears.

Noah tried to pull water from the lake to toss it over the Manticore, but the journey over in the boat had exhausted him, and no matter how much he tried, the water wouldn't do what he wanted. The Manticore placed all four feet on the ground, making the ground shake, and lifted its tail like a scorpion. And then it shot a huge spike directly at them.

"Watch out!" Ava screamed. The spike was coming right for Mason.

Suddenly the spike burst into flames and fell to the ground. But another one followed, and then another, aimed at all four of them. It seemed like the Manticore was never going to run out of spikes, like they were re-growing instantaneously.

They ducked and dodged and tried to move around. But almost like it was in another world entirely, a bright blue butterfly landed on the Manticore's head.

"That's it! I have an idea," Sophia said, moving close to Noah. She shoved the blue crystal in his hand. "You see the butterfly?"

"Yeah," Noah said.

"It's touching the monster. That's what we need to do," Sophia said.

"We need to land on its head?" Noah said.

"No. But we do need to make contact," Sophia said. "I'll distract it with fire while you sneak around. Touch the monster with the crystal. That has to be how we capture it."

"That's too dangerous," Noah said. "I'll distract it instead."

"Your magic isn't working right now," Sophia said.

Noah hated that she was right, but her logic made sense. If he couldn't use magic, then this was how he could be most useful.

Underneath them, the ground shook. Noah snapped his head to the Manticore, but it shook its massive head and looked around, like it was trying to figure out what had happened also.

"Mason!" Noah said.

Mason nodded and the ground shook again. "I'll help distract it."

Just then a burst of air whooshed past them and the Manticore's massive mane of hair blew all over its face, disorienting it. Ava gave him a thumbs up.

Noah had to take the chance.

He fell back, hiding behind the others, and tried to move as quickly as he could without drawing attention. The beach was wide open but the trees behind the Manticore could cover him. And then, from there, if he could reach the rocks, he would be so close.

Sophia continued to burn the spikes with her fire. Ava made the lion's mane blow in every direction. And Noah crept around, until he was right behind the giant beast. Its tail lashed backward and forward as it threw the spikes. Its skin shone and reflected the fire from Sophia. It roared and screamed and then, even though Noah had been so quiet, it whipped around until it faced him.

That's when the Manticore opened its mouth. Three horrible rows of teeth, sparkly white, shone back at Noah. And then it moved right for him. It was really going to eat him.

CHAPTER 13

Noah braced himself for the teeth. He clenched the crystal in one hand. Even if it ate him, maybe he could still capture it in the crystal.

"I'm not scared of you!" Noah screamed, even though he completely was scared of the monster. He had never, not even in any of the video games he liked, seen anything like it.

The mouth was only inches away. This was it. This was the end.

But then the ground collapsed underneath the Manticore and the monster dropped, falling into the earth. Noah didn't look around or wait. He jumped out and touched the blue crystal to the Manticore's head, right where the blue butterfly had landed.

Instantly it sucked the monster in, like a giant blob of food being sucked through a straw. The Manticore screamed as the crystal did its work, and then the screaming stopped. The Manticore was trapped. They'd done it. They'd captured the monster.

The crystal warmed in Noah's hand and then cast a blue light around them, lighting up the entire island. He held it high and they all watched and waited, until the light finally went out.

"We need to get it back to the Octo-thing," Mason said.

"Octolith," Sophia said.

"Yeah, Octolith," Mason said. "Maybe one of these days I'll remember that."

They found a boat on the island that hadn't been destroyed. Maybe the Manticore itself had used it to travel over and eat the pigs and cows. Or maybe it had been left by Crazy Joe. Regardless, the trip back took less time and they didn't end up falling into the water and almost being eaten by a giant fish.

They only stopped in the town long enough to let Jessie know what had happened.

"Make sure you tell everyone that wizards are back," Mason said to her.

"Yeah, Wizards of Tomorrow," Sophia said.

It had a great ring to it, almost like they were some sort of rock band.

From the town, they traveled back by the rock where the monkeys had been, but there was no sign of the three of them.

"Where do you think they went?" Noah asked.

"No idea," Ava said.

"Maybe they're off monkeying around," Mason said.

All three of them groaned at the bad pun.

They used their phone map app to retrace their steps back to the castle. They ducked inside the tunnel and hurried down the corridor until they came back to the room with the fireplace. Noah was about to pull the tapestry aside so they could go through the secret door, except he stopped.

"The monkeys aren't on the tapestry either," he said.

"Then how will we know where to find them?" Mason asked.

"We'll know," Sophia said. "Next time we're here, we'll know." She stepped forward and opened the door.

Inside was the Octolith. Noah immediately walked over to it and held the blue crystal near one of the empty sockets. The crystal snapped into place, glowing for only a moment before solidly seating itself. Noah tried to move it after that, but it wouldn't budge. And then, the world shifted. The walls around them turned gray and cloudy and everything went out of focus. The next thing Noah knew, he was back in his bedroom, holding his phone.

"That was your last warning!" his mom said, banging on his door.

Noah checked the clock. Quinn had been totally wrong. Over fifteen minutes had passed! And his mom had given him ten.

The door to his room flew open and in stormed his mom.

"Give me your phone," his mom said, holding her hand out. Next to her, his dog Xena barked and ran over to the bed.

"But Mom," Noah said. He glanced at the screen. The *Wizards of Tomorrow* app home screen was still loaded, but there was a message on the screen.

> Wizard of Tomorrow
> app currently
> UPDATING.

Would that message go away when it was time to go back and hunt the next monster? Noah had no idea. And without his phone, what would happen? His friends needed him.

"But Mom what?" his mom said. "Because unless you have a really good excuse, like the world was ending, then you lose your phone."

"I do have a good excuse," Noah said, and he vowed to let Quinn know about the time passing the next time he saw the game designer. If he ever had a chance. Without his phone, he would never travel back to the future.

"I'm waiting," his mom said.

Xena barked again, like she was waiting, too.

"There was this game I was playing," Noah started.

The look on his mom's face let him know how well that excuse was going to go over.

"I had to save the world!" Noah said.

"Really?" Disbelief covered her face.

"It's true. I went to the future and there was magic and monsters and . . ." His voice trailed off. This was never going to work.

"One week without your phone," his mom said and she held her hand out.

Just then the phone buzzed with an incoming message on the *Wizards of Tomorrow* home screen. It was from Mason. Noah barely had time to glance at it.

Mason: Are you guys there?

Sophia: I'm back! Coolest thing ever!

Ava: It wasn't so bad.

Sophia: Noah???

Noah held his finger over the screen. He needed to say something or else they'd go ahead without him. But he never got a chance.

"One week," his mom said, and she snatched the phone from his hand.

Mason: When do you think we go back?

Ugh. This was the worst. And it was only the first day of Spring Break. That meant he was going to be stuck the entire time with no phone. No way to get back into the *Wizards of Tomorrow* app. As soon as his mom left the room, he was going to visit Sophia. She could at least pass messages back and forth for him.

"You missed out on laundry, but don't forget your other chores," his mom said. "Your room is a disaster."

His mom left and he flopped back on the bed. This was the worst.

Xena hopped up on the bed and started licking his face. Cleaning his room was the last thing he wanted to do, but if he didn't do it, he would only get in more trouble. And maybe, if he did a really good job, his mom would give him back the phone early.

He started on all the clothes scattered around the floor and over the chair and put all those away, then went to the dresser. He left his desk for last because it was covered in everything from Legos to dirty socks. While he was moving one of his Mini-figs, his hand brushed the mouse on his computer. The screen popped to life, and a window popped up on the screen.

Noah clicked YES.

The app started downloading.

A NOTE FROM CONNOR

To all the Wizards of Tomorrow out there:

Thank you so much for taking the time to read
Wizards of Tomorrow! It's wizards (and readers)
like you who will save the future!

If you did enjoy reading *Wizards of Tomorrow*,
I would love if you would take a few moments
to review the book on Amazon. Reviews are so
important these days, and even a one sentence
review can make a huge difference in other
readers discovering the series.

Now go and save the world
(or read another book)!

—CONNOR HOOVER

LOOKING FOR MORE
**WIZARDS
OF
TOMORROW?**

THE ADVENTURE
CONTINUES IN
**WIZARDS
OF
TOMORROW
BOOK 2,**
AVAILABLE NOW!

LIKE ADVENTURE STORIES?
THINK ALIENS ARE COOL?

LOOK FOR

A NEW SERIES
COMING FROM
CONNOR HOOVER!

SIGN UP FOR THE
LATEST NEWS HERE:

www.connorhoover.com

ABOUT THE AUTHOR

Connor Hoover wanted to be a wizard and wanted to time travel, but when that didn't work out, Connor wrote about time traveling wizards instead. It's actually pretty fun.

To contact Connor:

connor@connorhoover.com

www.connorhoover.com

Made in the USA
San Bernardino, CA
23 January 2018